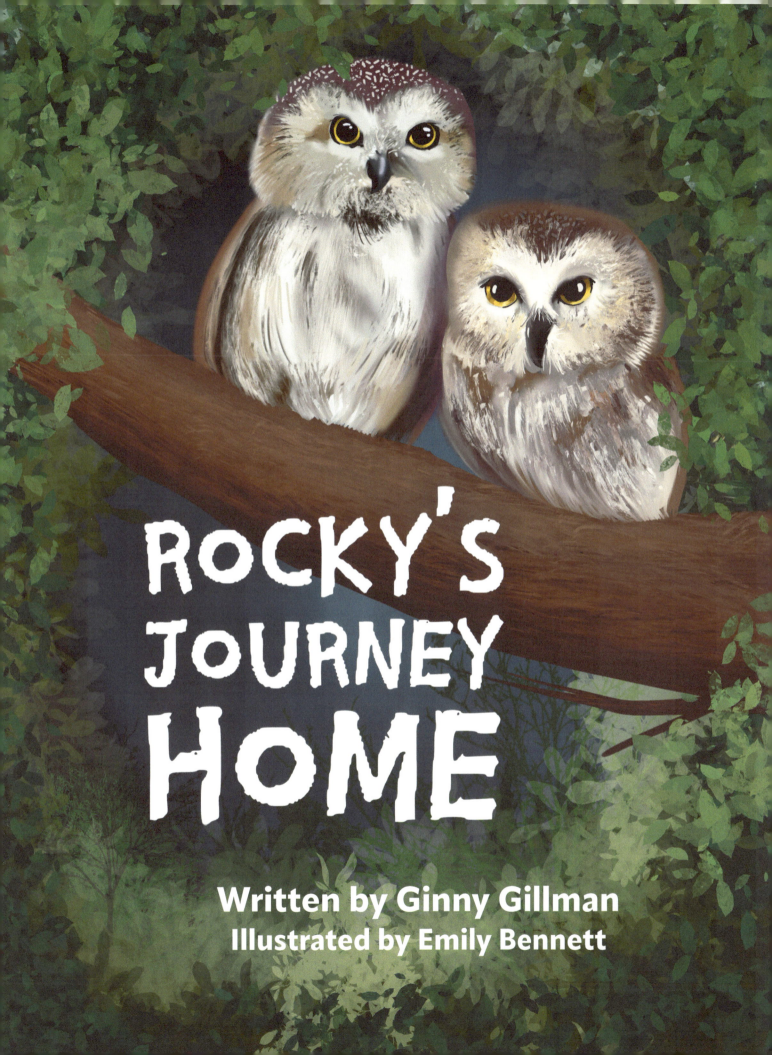

Copyright © 2024 Ginny Gillman

Illustrations copyright © 2024 Emily Bennett

September 2024

All rights reserved

No part of this book may be used or reproduced in any manner whatsoever without written permission from the author.

Printed in the United States of America

Library of Congress Control Number: 2024920129

ISBN: 979-8-89228-286-4 (Paperback)
ISBN: 979-8-89228-287-1 (Hardcover)
ISBN: 979-8-89228-288-8 (eBook)

This book belongs to:

Rocky was famous.

Do you know why?

This young saw-whet owl was discovered inside an abandoned woodpecker hole in New York City's Rockefeller Center Christmas tree as it was being decorated for the 2020 holiday. The Norwegian spruce was her "birth" tree, where she had hatched from an egg. Her story was so fun and popular that her portrait was painted on the tails of commercial airplanes.

Where is Rocky now?

Rocky lives in a hole in a cedar board attached to a house. The hole was made by a woodpecker whose babies grew too large for their nest. They flew away, allowing Rocky to move right in. Her little body filled the space perfectly.

But outside her cozy nest, the temperature was rising.

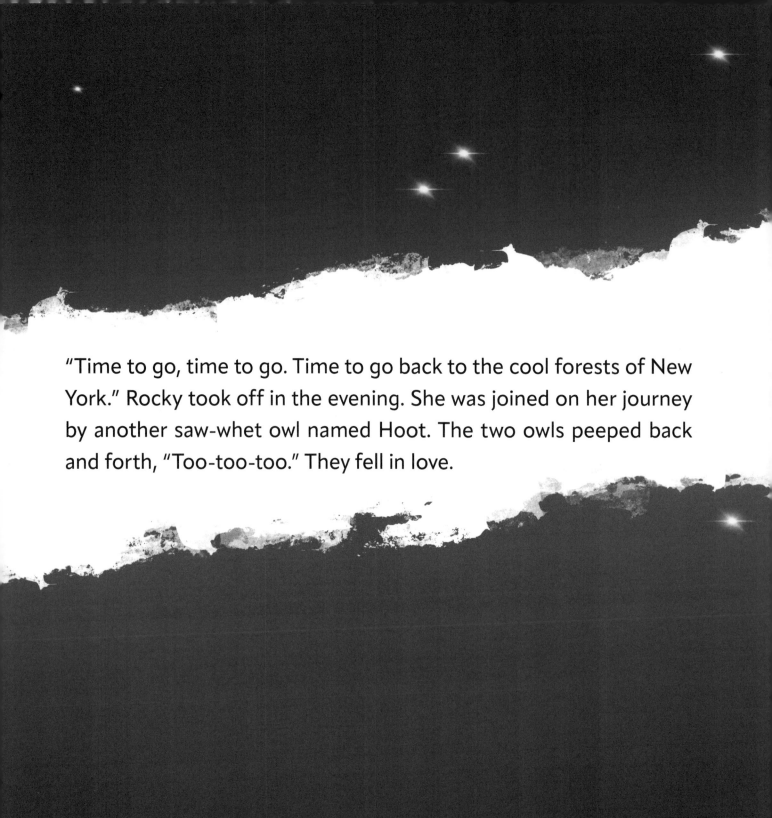

"Time to go, time to go. Time to go back to the cool forests of New York." Rocky took off in the evening. She was joined on her journey by another saw-whet owl named Hoot. The two owls peeped back and forth, "Too-too-too." They fell in love.

Rocky and Hoot flew into the familiar forest, where Rocky had been hatched.

There, they found a nesting spot in a pecked-out knothole in an old pine tree.

Rocky laid four precious eggs, each about the size of a large acorn. She sat on the eggs to keep them warm while Hoot hunted for their food.

After sitting on her eggs for almost one month, Rocky felt the eggs tickle her tummy feathers. Out popped four tiny, healthy, hungry owlets. Rocky happily hugged her babies.

One morning, Hoot did not return from his hunting.

"Skiew, skiew, skiew," his cries echoed from a distance.

There was danger nearby. A great horned owl, a forest predator, was looking for a meal. Rocky shivered with fear and spread her wings over her babies.

As the sun became brighter, human voices echoed in the forest. "Some of these old, dried pine trees need to be cut down," shouted a forest ranger.

Startled, the great horned owl spread his massive wings and glided away to seek food elsewhere. Hoot safely flew to the nest.

The ranger tied yellow tape around Rocky's pine tree and tagged it. It was a bad sign for the owl family because the old pine tree would have to be cut down.

The next day, a logger fired up his chain saw. Rocky and Hoot flew off to a nearby branch, leaving their babies behind. The owlets were too young to fly. Rocky and Hoot fluttered in a panic as they watched the logger cut down the pine tree.

The owl pair cried out, "Skiew, skiew, skiew!" Their warning cries could not be heard over the buzzing saw. The owl pair tried to distract the logger by flying helter-skelter above his head. They snapped their beaks and screeched.

As the pine trunk was dragged onto a truck bed, the logger shouted, "Looky here!" He bent over the log, reaching for the four shivering owlets. "Thank goodness we didn't cut through this nest."

The logger lifted the downy owlets out of the nesting hole and laid them into a cloth-lined pail. "I'll take these babies to Doctor Emily at the wildlife rescue center."

Rocky and Hoot flew frantically over the logger's truck as it rumbled toward the rescue center.

When the exhausted owl pair arrived at the rescue center, they perched nearby and peeked into the front window. Their hearts beat like snare drums.

Doctor Emily placed the babies into a glass cage so she could watch them. "I think I can save them," she announced to the logger.

To the owlets, she whispered, "You look very healthy. Your mother and father have taken good care of you."

At first, Doctor Emily had to pry open each owl's beak with a pair of tweezers in order to feed it small pieces of raw meat. She gently held each owl in her hand as its talons danced. Their beaks snapped at the food as they wiggled and chirped because Emily was not their mother. She was a stranger.

Soon, the owlets learned that Emily meant food and kindness. They opened their beaks easily as they were fed the meaty treats. As the brave owlets grew stronger, they fledged, stretching their wings and flying around the doctor's workspace. They perched on a wooden curtain rod for rest.

When the owlets were ready to live on their own, Doctor Emily brought them outdoors in a wire cage and unhooked the door. "I will miss you."

"Skiew, skiew, skiew!" they announced to the world as they flew off. Doctor Emily had given each owlet a secret name. She loved them so.

The bear cubs, butterflies, bugs, and bees welcomed the owlets back into the forest, which hummed with excitement. As Rocky and Hoot happily watched this touching moment, they tilted their heads together, knowing in their hearts that their babies were alive and well.

Will Rocky and Hoot find a new home?

They spotted a wooden box attached to a large oak tree. They flew around the box, curious about this strange object. The box had a hole on one side, just the right size for their feathery bodies. They squeezed inside and snuggled together. "Too-too-too," meaning, *"We will be safe here."*

The piney scent of the nesting box reminded Rocky of her Norwegian spruce "birth" tree. What she didn't know was that this box was stamped with welcoming words.

Rocky was home, indeed!

Ginny (Vergene) Gillman is a retired elementary school teacher. She is an "outdoors girl," who spends half the year in "green and gold" Wisconsin, and the other half in sunny and sandy Southern California. Ginny is a mother to two handsome sons and grandmother to three smart and talented grandchildren. Wherever she lands, you will find her golfing with Tom, riding her e-bike, relaxing with a good book, singing in the church choir, treading water in a local pool, and tapping away on her computer. *Rocky's Journey Home* is the sequel to her first book about *Rocky, The Christmas Stowaway*.

Emily Bennett is a high school science teacher and artist. She lives in Appleton where she enjoys restoring her 100-year old home and creating art.

She has always had a passion for science and art and believes that kids should be free to pursue multiple passions. Emily loves utilizing her science background in her art and taking the time to truly understand the details of her subject matter.

Questions for Rocky's Journey Home:

1. Why was Rocky famous?
2. Where was Rocky living at the beginning of the story?
3. Why did she decide to fly back to the forest?
4. How many owlets hatched in the nest? Count them.
5. What large owl was mentioned in the story?
6. Why were Rocky and Hoot so afraid?
7. Who saved the baby owlets?
8. What special tool was used to feed the owlets?
9. If you could be any character in the story, who would you wish to be?
10. What was the nesting box made of?
11. What names would YOU give to the four baby owlets?
12. Tell the story in your own words, looking at the pictures.

The Great Horned Owl

The great horned owl is one of the largest owls in nature. If compared to a saw-whet owl, this big fellow is three to six times larger than four to six inch tall saw-whet. As suggested in the name, this owl has large ear tufts for greater listening. Its strong talons take down prey much larger than itself. Great horned owls live in a variety of locations in North America.

Milton Keynes UK
Ingram Content Group UK Ltd.
UKHW050306211024
449849UK00008B/45